Before You Were Born

Written by Nancy White Carlstrom

Illustrated by Linda Saport

Eerdmans Books for Young Readers

Grand Rapids, Michigan • Cambridge, U.K.

Text © 2002 Nancy White Carlstrom
Illustrations © 2002 Linda Saport

Published 2002 by Eerdmans Books for Young Readers
An imprint of Wm. B. Eerdmans Publishing Company
255 Jefferson S.E., Grand Rapids, Michigan 49503
P.O. Box 163, Cambridge CB3 9PU U.K.

Library of Congress-in-Publication Data
Carlstrom, Nancy White.
Before You Were Born / written by Nancy White Carlstrom;
illustrated by Linda Saport.
p. cm.
Summary: A poetic recounting of how the birth of a child
changes the lives of the parents.
 ISBN 0-8028-5185-1 (alk. paper)
 [1. Babies—Fiction. 2. Parent and child—Fiction.]
I. Saport, Linda, ill. II. Title.
PZ7.C21684 Be 2002
[E]—dc21   2001040173

The illustrations were rendered in charcoal and pastel on paper.
The display type was set in Pablo.
The text type was set in Cantoria.
Book design by Jesi Josten.

The scripture quotation is taken from the Holy Bible,
New International Version®, NIV®
Copyright 1973, 1978, 1984 by International Bible Society.
Used by permission of Zondervan Publishing House.

For my family, with love
— N.W.C.

Especially for Jim and Sue Elder
— L.S.

Before you were born
God wrote your days in a book.

And when you arrived
the moon
dusted the hills
with a fine bright snow.

We wrapped you in white
and introduced you to the dawn.

Before you were born
we watched the ducks stand on their heads
in the golden pond
while the sun flamed red
behind the apple orchard.

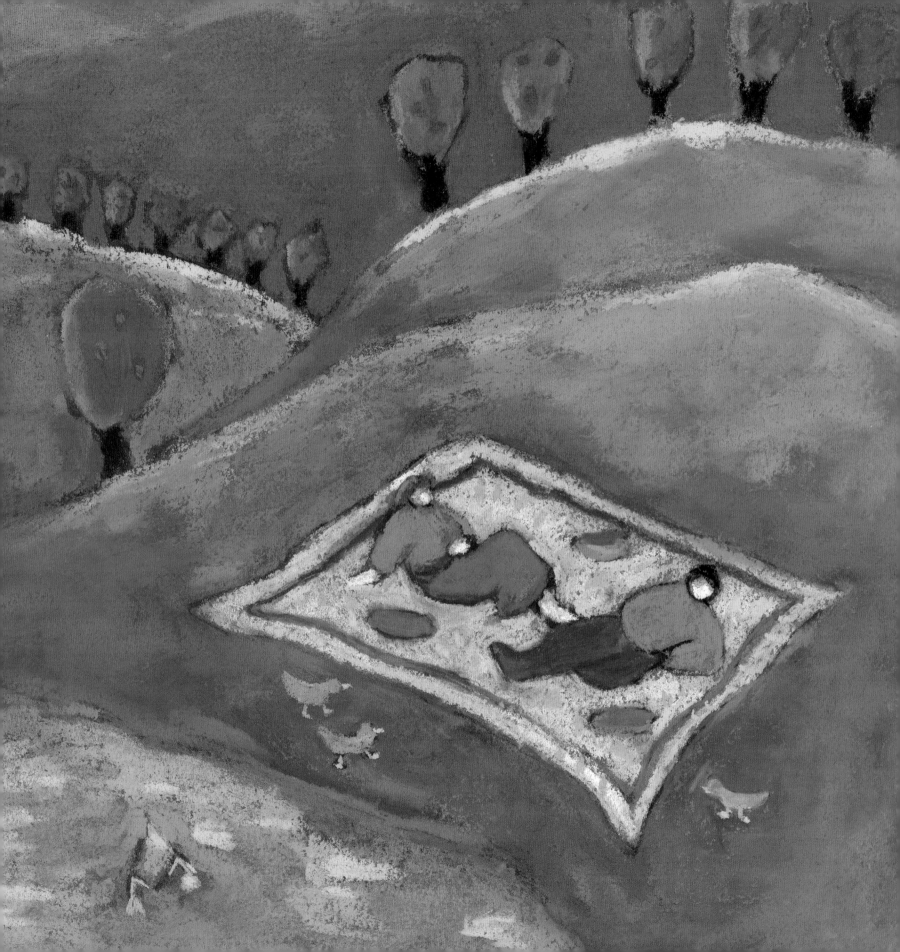

But when you arrived
our eyes were only on you
glowing in the bed between us.

The entire duck family quacked
in celebration
as fire spread across the sky
and you were our delight.

Before you were born
the cat played with strings
and the little dog laughed.

But when you arrived
we showed you
your own silver spoon
and a yellow dish,

and even the cat and dog
seemed to know
you were well worth the wait.

Before you were born
we threw bread to the fish
who came to the surface
of the water shining like a mirror.

But when you arrived
we whispered your name,
and the rainbow trout
wished you well
and sent colors.

And we were all shining.

Before you were born
Great Grandmama
from over the hill
brought a tiny cap
woven of silk and moonbeams.

For baby dreams, she said.

But when you arrived
she held you in her ancient arms
singing
and the years between you and her
were greater even than the years
we three carried all together.

Her blessing song was like a star
rising to the heavens.
God must have smiled.

Before you were born
we could tell when things would happen,
plan what to do, where to go.

But when you arrived
the Christmas cactus burst into bloom
nine months early or three months late
and the mail brought two cards for you
right on time.

How did they know?

Before you were born
we thought we knew
the hours of the brown owls in the woods
and the seasons of the creatures.

But when you arrived
even the old groundhog
walked out of his winter sleep
to greet you.

Before you were born
we thought we were writing
our own days in a book.

But when you arrived
we tiptoed through faraway shadows
and your late afternoon nap
so that your waking cries
could keep us up
all the starry-dark night.

And we didn't even mind.

For we wanted those minutes and hours
to be written firmly upon our memory.

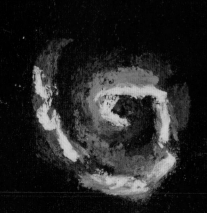

So as years and years and years
pass by
and the land and the sky
and the woods all around change —
and we do too —
our love for you
will be worn the same way
only more.

And we can say
we know full well
that before you were born
God wrote your days in a book
and sent you to us.

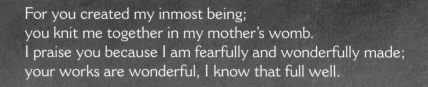

For you created my inmost being;
you knit me together in my mother's womb.
I praise you because I am fearfully and wonderfully made;
your works are wonderful, I know that full well.

My frame was not hidden from you
when I was made in the secret place.
When I was woven together in the depths of the earth,
your eyes saw my unformed body.

All the days ordained for me were written
in your book before one of them came to be.

Psalm 139: 13-16